A HUGH DUNNIT MYSTERY

TAKING SHELTER

STORY BY
GUY BASS

ILLUSTRATIONS BY
LEE COSGROVE

Andersen Press

A HUGH DUNNIT MYSTERY

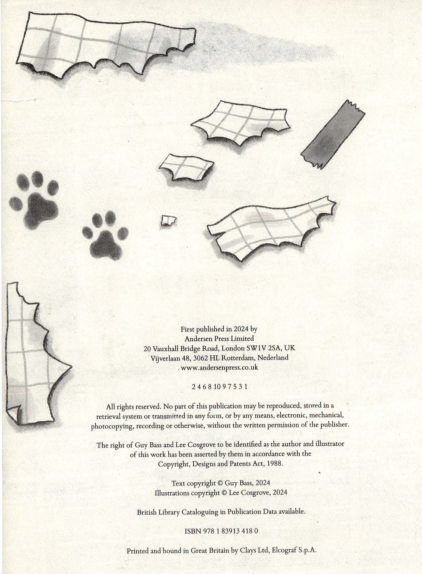

First published in 2024 by
Andersen Press Limited
20 Vauxhall Bridge Road, London SW1V 2SA, UK
Vijverlaan 48, 3062 HL Rotterdam, Nederland
www.andersenpress.co.uk

2 4 6 8 10 9 7 5 3 1

British Library Cataloguing in Publication Data available.

ISBN 978 1 83913 418 0

Printed and bound in Great Britain by Clays Ltd, Elcograf S.p.A.

1.

Shelter

This case . . . this *crime*. Where to start?

I guess I should begin at the beginning, and work back from there.

Yesterday, otherwise known as Tuesday, I was in the park. Rain had started to fall. It was heavier than my tummy after a baked potato, so I picked up my bag and took Shelter under a tree. Shelter's the name of my dog. She's my best friend. She's the only person I trust in the whole world, and she isn't a person, she's a Staffordshire bull terrier.

Shelter's called Shelter because that's where I found her – a bus shelter. That was almost a month ago. It was raining on the day we met,

too. The rain hit the ground like soggy fists. I was on my way home from school. I ran to the bus shelter for cover . . . and that's when I spotted her. She was spotted – two of them, on her rump. Her spots were as white as good teeth, but the rest of her was greyer than a bad mood. She huddled in a corner, trying to stay dry, and possibly waiting for the Number 13 bus. I took one look at her, and she took one look at me. Then she took another look at me, exactly the same as before. *I know that look*, I thought.

As soon as I picked her up, I could feel we had a connection. Turns out she'd got her claws snagged on my coat. But more than that, I just

had a feeling. In that moment, I knew this dog was going to be my best friend. I picked her up and sneezed. Turns out I'm allergic to dog hair. Allergies really get up my nose. But that didn't stop me carrying Shelter home.

After a bit more sneezing, I explained to Dad what had happened. Then Mum came home and I explained all over again. I hate having to repeat myself. Seriously, I hate having to repeat myself.

Anyway, Mum and Dad said I couldn't just take a dog. Which was ridiculous, because that was what I'd just done. I had to put up posters all over the village to check if Shelter's owners were looking for her. I made them myself.

Mum and Dad made me take them all down.
Then they put up their own, which just said:

DOG FOUND
Call: 01632 555 751

. . . But no one called. Mum said we should take Shelter to the shelter. I said, Why would I take her back there? Mum said, No, the *dog* shelter. I said I know Shelter's a dog. I was stalling. I knew there was only a faint chance I could keep her, but I wasn't holding my breath. So I held my breath until I fainted.

After I woke up, Mum said I could keep Shelter as long as she didn't cause any trouble. I said, What do you mean, trouble? Mum said, You know what I mean. I said, What do you mean, I know what you mean? Then Mum made that noise she makes when she doesn't want to say words any more. Dad shook his head. I sneezed.

And that's how I ended up with my best friend.

But this isn't the story of how I found Shelter.

This is the story of how I lost her.

2.

The Crime

They say there's no such thing as victimless crime. But what about blowing up a ghost? They're already dead.

But *this* crime did have a victim . . . and that victim was me. I didn't even see it coming. When bad things happen, they don't often let you know they're on their way. They sneak up on you like a soundproofed ninja in soft socks.

It was Wednesday. I was halfway through the week but my troubles had only just started. In the morning, I went downstairs, ate breakfast, and then headed back up to my bedroom to get my bag. It had my maths homework in it, and today was the day I had to hand it in.

Maths is my second favourite subject. I don't have a first – I don't like to choose favourites. Everybody knows I'm best at maths. Once, around six days, seven hours and forty-three minutes ago, my teacher, Miss Adwell, was talking us through a maths question in class.

'So, if we take this seven-sided shape,' she began, 'otherwise known as a . . . ?'

I put up my hand. Everyone looked down, like Miss Adwell's stare could turn them

8

to stone. My hand was still up when Miss Adwell added, 'Anyone? Connie B? You know this.'

'. . . Septagon?' said Connie Baffle.

I did not put my hand down.

'Good – Connie B is *Math-magician* of the Day,' said Miss Adwell. 'So, in order to calculate the area of—'

'Miss?' I said.

Miss Adwell's sigh sounded a bit like my mum's.

'. . . Hugh?' she said.

'A seven-sided polygon is called a heptagon,' I said.

Another sigh. That one sounded a *lot* like my mum's.

'Both are acceptable, Hugh,' said Miss Adwell.

'But a heptagon is from the Greek "heptá" and septagon is from Latin "septa" but all other polygon names come from Greek, so—'

'*Both are acceptable, Hugh,*' Miss Adwell said

again. She sounded like she wanted the ground to swallow me up, but I just sat there, so I guess the ground wasn't hungry. But the fact was, I knew I was right, and Miss Adwell knew I was right, and everyone in the class knew I was right.

Something impossible had happened, and it had happened to me.

I was righter than my teacher.

Miss Adwell just carried on with the lesson, but I could tell she was shaken. Her whole world had come crashing down around her ears, and I'd swung the wrecking ball. I could have lived in that moment for a week. Apart from meeting Shelter and that time I discovered I could raise one eyebrow, it was the best thing that ever happened to me.

The point is, I'm good at maths – copy-my-homework good. I'd already done my homework in Tuesday's lunch break, so I'd have more time to play with Shelter after school. Home is no place for homework.

Anyway, as I was saying, I went back to my room after breakfast, and there it was.

Not in my bag, on my bedroom floor. My homework was *all over* my bedroom floor.

And it was torn to shreds.

I'd spent a whole hour on it. Well, half an hour. The point is, I worked hard on that homework for a full thirteen minutes, and then, on the morning I had to hand it in, I found it ripped into considerably more than a hundred tiny pieces.

I was in trouble . . . but little did I know, my troubles had just begun.

'Hugh, school! Do you want a lift or not?' Mum shouted in her shouting voice. 'Do not make me late!'

Mum is a tennis coach. I don't know much about tennis, but Mum knows how to make a racket.

Before I knew it, she'd appeared in the doorway.

'Coat. Bag. Car. Now,' Mum said. 'I cannot be late agai— Oh, not *again*! Is – is that your homework?'

'*Was*,' I replied, inspecting the tattered paper. I could see random parts of numbers and equations. 'It used to be my maths homework, but now something doesn't add up,' I added. 'Who did this?'

'What do you mean, who did— You know full well who did this!' Mum howled. She isn't usually one to point the finger, but today it pointed straight in the direction of my best friend.

I couldn't believe what I was hearing.

'Who, Shelter?' I asked, also not able to believe that I was saying what I think my mum was saying. Shelter barked at the sound of her name. She probably couldn't believe what she was hearing either.

'What are you saying? That Shelter ate my homework?' I asked, now not able to believe my own disbelief.

'Oh, come on,' Mum said, throwing up her arms. 'It's not like she doesn't have previous form when it comes to getting her teeth into things . . .'

'She wouldn't,' I said, staring at the scraps of paper on the floor. 'She wouldn't do that.'

'She *has* done that,' Mum replied. 'She's chewed my shoes. She's shredded my bed. She's munched my lunch.'

'But—'

'She's gnawed my keyboard, my cheeseboard, the floorboards . . . and what's worse, she ate my purse! All that money! Do you think it's funny?' Mum continued. 'The *whole house* is covered in teeth marks, Hugh. This is the last straw – and she chewed my last straw! It's not even like she's our dog – not really.'

'She *is* our dog,' I corrected her, with a stifled sneeze. 'She's *my* dog.'

'And I told you, Hugh, if we had one more "incident", she was going to have to go.'

The pause hung in the air like damp laundry.

'Go?' I repeated. 'Go, where?'

'You know where,' Mum replied. Her words were as sharp as scissors, and her meaning was as blunt as safety scissors. 'If you – if *we* can't cope with her,' she continued, 'then we'll have to take Shelter to . . . the shelter.'

'No!' I protested. I glanced down at Shelter. If you believe what you read, dogs can understand up to one hundred-and-sixty-five words. I hoped Shelter wasn't paying attention.

'It wasn't her, Mum,' I said. 'She didn't do it. She *didn't*.'

'Then who did, Hugh?'

'I – I . . .'

'Exactly,' interrupted Mum. She tutted and rubbed her eyes. She looked tired, like an old jumper or a song no one plays any more. 'Let's get you to school,' she said at last. 'But this conversation is not over, Hugh.'

And just like that, the conversation was over. Mum didn't say a word on the way to the car, but she'd already said it all. Her words rang in my head like an unanswered telephone. They made my blood boil and chilled me to the core. Mum wanted to get rid of my best friend. I couldn't let that happen. That's when I realised, I had to clear Shelter's name. Just after that, I realised I had to do more than clear Shelter's name. Not only did I have to prove that Shelter had nothing to do with destroying my homework, I had to find out who did – I had to bring the real culprit to justice.

As we drove to school, I glanced in the rear-view mirror. *There's no looking back*, I thought. It was up to me to solve the Crime.

I was on the case.

3.

On the Case

IT WASN'T GOING TO BE EASY — THE HARD CASES NEVER ARE.

RIGHT NOW, I HAD TO SUSPECT EVERYONE WAS A SUSPECT. ALL I HAD WERE QUESTIONS. WHO DID THE CRIME?

AND WHY?

AND HOW?

AND WHEN?

AND WHO?

HUGH?

LIKE A MONKEY WITH A COCONUT, I HAD TO BUST THIS THING WIDE OPEN.

HUGH, ARE YOU LISTENING TO ME?

I was so busy not listening to Miss Adwell that I didn't hear her ask if I was listening to her. That's when she told me that not listening wasn't an option. At least I think that's what she said – I wasn't really listening. But *then* she cut to the chase.

'Your homework, Hugh,' she said, pointing to a stack of exercise books on her desk. 'Where is it?'

'I don't want to talk about it,' I said.

Four minutes later, Miss Adwell told me to stop talking about it.

'But it's a *crime*,' I explained again. 'C-R-I-M-E,' I added. Clearly, I needed to spell it out to her. 'My homework was destroyed, and I'm going to find out who did it.'

'Yes, you mentioned that, Hugh – *several times*. Can we move on, now?' Miss Adwell said as the rest of class laughed their judgemental laugh. They might not have taken my case seriously, but I knew that this crime was going to take some serious solving.

So far, I knew that the only thing I knew was that I didn't know anything. That was good to know. But when you're solving a crime, you learn to ignore your head and go with your gut, and my gut was telling me to use my head. There had to be a simple explanation for all this, but the simplest explanation can be the hardest to swallow. I had a hunch this was going to be harder to swallow than my gran's home-made cough medicine with the bits in it.

By the end of the day, I'd drawn a blank. Then again, I never was very good at drawing. Dad met me after school and gave me Shelter so I could take her to the park for a walk.

'Dinner's on the table at six-forty-five,' said Dad as we headed off. 'Wait, let's make it quarter to seven.'

Walking Shelter never involves much walking. Shelter likes to play Fetch. And by Fetch, I mean I throw her a ball and then she chews it until it's not a ball any more. As I watched her reduce her latest doomed sphere to its individual atoms, Mum's words echoed round my head like a long fart.

'*We'll have to take Shelter to the shelter.*'

How could Mum even be thinking about getting rid of Shelter? She was house-trained, didn't drool, licked your face when she was excited – everything you could want out of a best friend. I couldn't imagine life without my dog. I couldn't even imagine imagining it. As far as I was concerned, Shelter was part of the family.

Suddenly, a thought hit my brain like a fly on a windscreen.

Him.

How could I not have seen it earlier? It was the only possible explanation. It was him all along. He did it!

It was time to pay him a visit.

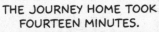

THE JOURNEY HOME TOOK FOURTEEN MINUTES.

THE TRIP UPSTAIRS TOOK ELEVEN SECONDS,

BUT ONLY COS SHELTER STOPPED TO CHEW THINGS OVER.

I COULD FEEL MY HEART PUMPING IN MY TOES AS I GOT TO THE LAST DOOR ON THE LANDING.

I DIDN'T BOTHER TO KNOCK.

ALSO, THE DOOR WAS OPEN.

IT WAS **YOU**, WASN'T IT? DON'T BOTHER TRYING TO DENY IT.

I NEED A CONFESSION TO CLEAR MY FRIEND'S NAME, SO YOU'D BETTER START **SINGING LIKE A CANARY.**

IT LOOKED LIKE HE WASN'T IN THE MOOD TO TALK, EITHER.
THEN AGAIN, MY BROTHER IS ONLY EIGHTEEN MONTHS OLD.

'Taa pah,' said my brother.

I had a feeling I didn't need my brushes – he got the picture, all right. Sure, I wasn't about to get any sense out of him, and he definitely wasn't about to come clean – not with that smell coming from his nappy.

This stinks, I thought. My hunch had been right all along. My own brother, trying to frame my dog for a crime she didn't commit. Was it jealousy? Did he resent Shelter's superior bowel control? I looked down at my best friend, who looked back with her 'I knew you could do it' look. I scratched her ear, safe in the knowledge she was in the clear. I guess in the end, that's all that mattered. I'd caught the culprit. I'd solved the crime.

Case closed, I thought.

Or so I thought.

4.

A Spanner in the Works

'Let me get this straight,' said Mum, after I debriefed her and Dad about Ivor's misdemeanours. Even though I'd given it to them straight, Mum looked bent out of shape. 'You're saying your *brother* ate your homework.'

'Yep,' I said. 'I mean, you saw the mess. There wasn't much left. I'm not sure how much he actually swallowed.'

Mum shook her head. *This must be hard for her to swallow,* I thought.

'You're trying to tell us your eighteen-month-old brother escaped from his cot, crept into your room, ripped your homework to shreds and snuck back to his cot without anyone noticing?' Mum continued. Her voice was two parts doubt and one part suspicion, with just a dash of uncertainty. Was she looking for holes in my case? She took off her glasses and polished them. I could tell she couldn't see what was right in front of her, so I turned to Dad.

'I know this must be hard to hear, but it's true – it's the only possible explanation,' I said.

Dad cleared his throat and shook his head – I had a bad feeling he was about to throw a spanner in the works. Turns out he had a whole box full of spanners, and he'd been practising his aim.

'The thing is, Hugh,' he began, 'Ivor wasn't upstairs when you were having breakfast. He was on the play mat in the front room.'

'. . . The play mat?' I repeated. I felt cold and hot at the same time, like a sink with both taps on. For a second, I wondered if Ivor could have managed to crawl to the bottom of the stairs, climb to the top and then jimmy the child lock without arousing suspicion.

No *way, baby,* I thought. The truth, like a sweaty wrestler, was hard to get to grips with, but Dad was right – my brother had an alibi. It couldn't have been him.

'I know what you're doing, Hugh,' said Dad with a sigh, giving Shelter's head a rub. 'But even if you weren't allergic to dogs, Shelter is—'

'I'm not allergic, it's hay fever,' I said with a sneeze. It was a lie, and Dad saw through me like I was a window.

'Even without your allergy, we're finding it hard to cope with Shelter,' Dad continued. 'We've tried our best – goodness knows, I've tried to train her not to chew everything in sight. But—'

'But we've run out of options,' Mum interrupted. I felt my jaw and my buttocks clench at the same time. 'Do you understand what we're saying, Hugh?'

I didn't answer, but I knew exactly what they were saying. But I knew something else too.

Something I knew they knew I knew.

I knew that whoever destroyed my homework was still on the loose . . . and only I could catch them.

When you're solving a crime, you have to start at the beginning . . . but I'd already been to the beginning and back again, and it had got me nowhere. My prime suspect was in the clear. Like a hungry fisherman, I had to widen my net. I needed a clue to help me get to the bottom, and hopefully top and sides, of who destroyed my homework.

I cast my mind back to Tuesday. I remembered it like it was yesterday, because it was.

Dad met me from school and went home, while I headed to the park with Shelter. A bunch of other kids from school were there. I left my bag by the swings. The swings are my favourite thing about the park. Sure, we've had our ups and downs, but who hasn't?

The point is, I played Fetch with Shelter until it started to rain. Before I took Shelter to take shelter under the tree, I collected my bag. It was just where I'd left it, as if nothing had changed . . . as if nothing had happened.

Then it hit me, like a badly thrown frisbee.

Something *had* happened. In fact, some*one* had happened.

Her name was Pearl.

5.

Pearl

Pearl had been my over-the-road neighbour since I remember having an over-the-road neighbour, and, apparently, for a bit before that. My mum and dad and her mum and dad were friends in the way that old people are friends because they can see in each other's windows, not because they have anything in common. But Pearl and I would *never* be friends. I didn't trust Pearl as far as I could throw her into a river. She was the sort of girl who'd be nice just so she could be twice as nasty – the sort of girl who'd ask to take your hand and then, when you weren't looking, bite it off. I tried to imagine what it would be like to suddenly have no hand, but I was stumped.

How could I not have seen it sooner? If anyone was going to destroy my homework, it was Pearl.

I already had the 'why' – after school, Pearl had asked if she could copy my homework.

'I know you've already done yours,' she said.

'Oh, really?' I replied, suspiciously. 'And how could you possibly know that?'

'Because I saw you do it at lunchtime,' she said. 'And then you told everybody you'd done it.'

Can't argue with you there, I thought.

'Can't argue with you there,' I said. 'But that doesn't mean I'm giving it to you. If I do, your homework will be the same as my homework.'

'I'll change some stuff. Miss Adwell will never know,' she said. I knew she was lying cos words were coming out of her mouth. 'Ugh, look, I only need it for five seconds – I'll just take a picture of it on my phone. ***Pleeeeeeease* . . .'**

It was the sort of 'pleeeeease' that would come back to haunt me, like a ghostly boomerang. But if I said no, I knew Pearl would never forgive me.

'No,' I said.

'But—'

'No.'

'Hugh, don't be—'

'No.'

And that was that, or so I thought. Pearl called me a stink-panted idiot-head, but words can't hurt me, unless they're painted on a sword. I didn't give it another thought, until I thought: She did it. It *had* to be Pearl who destroyed my homework – it was the only possible explanation. But how?

Of course.

The park.

Yesterday, when I'd taken Shelter to the park. Pearl and her friends were there too. They were hanging out by the swings without actually swinging on them – talk about not getting in the swing of things. Pearl must have seen my backpack and remembered my homework was in there. While I was busy watching my best friend commit ball murder, she reached into my bag, grabbed my homework, and took a photo on her phone so she could copy it later.

The perfect crime.

Then came the rain. I went back for my bag and Pearl slinked off into the woods behind the park. She went home and copied my homework, eager to pass it off as her own. Except Pearl knew that Miss Adwell wasn't an idiot (not like Mr Dunderhead.) The more she thought about it, the more Pearl realised that Miss Adwell would be able to *tell* that she'd copied my homework. She couldn't shake the fear of being found out. I had a feeling Pearl didn't sleep a wink. (Although if it's a wink it's already a bad sleep – it needs to be at least a blink, or you've still got one eye open.) Either way, Pearl knew that if she was going to get away with copying my homework, she'd have to cover her tracks. And that meant getting rid of the evidence. And that meant committing the crime right under, or at least relatively near, my nose.

By the time I went back upstairs to get my bag, she was long gone.

Pearl. Of course it was Pearl all along!

Case closed.

But that didn't mean my problems were over. What now? Confront her? Sure, Pearl liked to talk – she could talk a kettle into boiling – but was she about to confess to her crime? Not a chance. I knew I'd get more sense out of my brother, and he can't even say his own name. If I tried to convince Pearl to talk, she'd clam up like a mussel. But I had to let Mum and Dad know Shelter was innocent.

I had to let everyone know.

I had to send a message.

6.

The Message

'Hugh Dunnit, what did you do?' my mum asked, the vein on her forehead working overtime.

I still had the chalk in my hand.

'I did what I had to – I sent a message,' I replied. There was no point in pretending I hadn't written those words in giant letters on the drive over the road, especially since I'd signed my name.

I knew Mum wouldn't understand. We were different, Mum and me, like chalk and a different colour chalk. Dad didn't understand either, but I don't think he was even sure what had happened.

'Hugh, Hugh, Hugh . . .' he sighed, as if there were three of me, and he was disappointed in all of them. 'You just can't go around writing on the neighbours' wall.'

'*Drive*,' said Mum.

'Drive, where?' asked Dad. Mum grunted.

'No, I mean he wrote on their— Never mind.' Mum sighed and turned back to me with *that* look. 'More to the point, you simply cannot go around accusing people of things they didn't do, Hugh.'

'But she did do,' I said. I looked down at Shelter, who made that puffing noise she makes when she totally agrees with me. 'It's the only possible explanation.'

'You're really trying to tell us that the only explanation for your ruined homework is that Pearl *climbed up the wall of the house* so she could sneak into your room and destroy your homework?' Mum barked. I had a feeling it was one of those questions where she didn't actually want an answer.

'Yes,' I answered. 'Case closed.'

Mum and Dad both sat back in their chairs and flared their nostrils like I was a bad smell on a hot day.

'Hugh Dunnit, you're going to stop with all this "case" nonsense right this minute, do you understand?' said Mum at last. I could tell she was angry. Like a toddler building a snowman, I was going to have to use kid gloves.

'I—' was all I managed. It turned out Mum wasn't in the mood for an answer, in case she didn't get the one she wanted. 'Right now, you're going to go over the road and say sorry to Pearl,' she went on, 'and you're going to apologise to her mum and dad while you're at it. *And* you're going to take a bucket of soapy water and a sponge with you. I want that drive spotless.'

A clean up job, I thought. *This is going to be dirty work.*

'But—' I began.

'And first thing tomorrow,' Mum added, 'your dad's going to call the dog shelter—'

'She only comes when *I* call,' I interrupted.

'No, not call the dog *Shelter*, call the dog shel— You know what I mean!' Mum snapped.

I did. I knew exactly what she meant.

Mum and Dad were trying to take me off the case.

Scrubbing the chalk off Pearl's drive didn't sound like much fun. Turns out it was as much fun as it sounded. Still, it gave me time to think. Mum had it in her head that my best friend was somehow

involved in the crime. She was willing to pin the whole thing on Shelter and send her to dog prison, which was bound to be rough. I knew Mum was barking up the wrong tree, but if I wanted to stop her from taking my dog, I had to prove it.

I had to find the *real* culprit, and fast.

As monstrous as Pearl was, maybe Mum was right – she didn't have the *brains* to carry out such a dastardly crime, never mind the teeth.

I admit I hated to admit it, but I had to admit, Pearl was in the clear.

That meant whoever destroyed my homework was still at large.

No suspects, no motives . . . that meant it could be anyone. Anyone on the street . . . anyone at school . . . anyone in the entire village. I wasn't sure where to start, but if I didn't start, I was finished. Once I'd scrubbed the drive and apologised to Pearl ('I'm sorry if you feel that I was wrong to accuse you') and her parents ('I'm sorry if you feel I was wrong to write on your drive'), Shelter and I set out looking for clues.

This village could be unforgiving – I could forgive it that. But someone had it in for Shelter, or me, or both of us.

Like an owl with a stuck neck, I was going to have to watch my back.

7.

A Breakthrough
(and a Break-in)

Shelter and I wandered the streets for what seemed like hours. Nine minutes later, we crossed the bridge to the posh side of the village.

As we passed by passersby, my mind raced faster than a dog chasing a cat chasing a mouse. If I didn't clear Shelter's name before tomorrow, I'd lose my best friend for ever. At this point, I wasn't even sure I could convince Mum and Dad to give her another chance, but if I didn't try, then . . .

My train of thought was derailed, like a car skidding off the road into a derailed train. I suddenly realised where we were – Number 22 Black Swan Spinney. Of course, it suddenly all made sense! Destiny had shown me the way. Destiny was a girl in my class who once pointed out the house when we were on the school bus, so I knew exactly who lived there.

Miss Adwell.

My teacher hadn't been in the village long. Mum said she didn't know how she could afford a place in the posh end of the village on a teacher's salary. She sure seemed like the sort of person to have secrets. Not like Mr Openbook.

Suddenly, it hit me like a tonne of things that each weighed a tonne. I'd been looking at the case all wrong. Staring up at that house, I could finally see the truth.

It was Miss Adwell who destroyed my homework.

Like holding a diary up to a mirror, I reflected on the events of the previous week.

AS THE MINUTES AND HOURS TICKED AWAY . . .

MISS ADWELL HAD BECOME **OBSESSED.**

SHE WAS HAUNTED BY MY VICTORY OVER HER.

SHE WAS **HUNGRY FOR VENGEANCE.**

AND OCCASIONALLY FOR BISCUITS.

Like that time I fell into the deep end of the pool, I suddenly felt out of my depth. I probably should have gone home. I probably should have told Mum and Dad what Miss Adwell had done. But what if they didn't believe me? What if they accused me of accusing Miss Adwell? I couldn't stand to stand accused – and chances are I'd be grounded quicker than a pigeon with two broken wings. I'd lose my last chance to clear Shelter's name.

Like a clown with a matchbox, I was playing with fire. But I had no choice – I had to handle this, here and now. I had to find proof, whatever the cost.

By now, it was starting to get dark. I knew the clock was ticking – I could see it through the window on Miss Adwell's mantelpiece. I had to have a proper look around, and make sure I wasn't discovered – last month, Miss Adwell did a whole assembly on how much she loved

karate. But if I could find something, *anything,* tying Miss Adwell to the crime, then Mum and Dad would have no choice but to let Shelter stay.

I took a deep breath. Then I sneezed, then I took another breath. There was no going back now. Shelter and I headed into the garden through the side gate and snuck round the back of the house.

While I got busy busily looking for clues, Shelter sniffed out a dog flap in the back door. Miss Adwell had a dog. This complicated things. My sneaking skills might just have been good enough to avoid a teacher with a purple belt in karate – but a dog with a nose built for sniffing and a jaw built for biting children?

That was another story, and the story ended with me getting at least slightly eaten. I was already heading back towards the side gate when Shelter suddenly made a beeline for the dog flap and leaped through it.

'Shelter, wait . . . !' I blurted, in the exact moment that Shelter did not wait. The flap creaked as it swung. She was inside the house. If I'd have known what I was doing, I would have told myself not to do what I did, but before I knew what I was doing, I'd done it.

I'd crawled through the dog flap.

8.

Like a Thief in a Ketchup Factory

I found myself in the kitchen. Well, mostly, since my bottom half was still on the other side of the dog flap. Miss Adwell's house smelled like fabric conditioner, but it was gloomier than a funeral – lights off and blinds drawn. It looked like no one was home, except, almost certainly, Miss Adwell's hungry dog. I squinted, scouring the room.

'Shelter? Shelter . . . !' I whispered, in a voice that I hoped was loud enough to call my own dog, but too quiet to alert Miss Adwell's child-eating hound. Nothing. I could hear the silence, and it sounded like trouble. I pulled the rest of my body through and crawled on my hands and knees across the kitchen. 'Shelter, where are you?'

More crawling took me to the kitchen doorway. By now I was half-looking for Shelter, half-looking for clues and half-wondering what I was still doing there. That made three halves. This time, something *definitely* didn't add up.

I poked my head out of the doorway and looked left. It felt like the right thing to do. Down the hall, right there on the left, was a set of stairs. Left of the stairs, right in front of me, was the front door. As I squinted in the gloom,

I saw a dark shape. I gasped so loudly I scared myself, and I was already more nervous than a pumpkin on Halloween.

Miss Adwell's dog!

Then I noticed it was grey. Just after that, I spotted the two spots on its rump.

So, not Miss Adwell's dog at all.

Mine. It was my dog.

Shelter was staring up at the door, as still as a statue of a dog staring at a door.

'Shelter . . . ! Shelter, what are you doing?' I hissed. I started crawling towards her with the sort of pace my little brother could only dream of, when the sound of a key turning in a lock told me that a key was turning in a lock. I panicked. Like a thief in a ketchup factory, I was about to be caught red-handed.

There was no time to grab Shelter. I dived into the gap under the stairs and froze like ice cream in the Arctic. Then I heard the door swing open.

Miss Adwell's scream was so loud it made my teeth hurt. For a second, I wondered if Shelter had leaped to my defence and pounced on her. I'd seen her chew a lot of things, but never a person. Like the captain of the Titanic, I had a sinking feeling. Then something happened that I couldn't have seen coming even if it had headlights. Miss Adwell said a single word.

'Mabel?'

Mabel? Who's Mabel? I thought. A new suspect, this late in the case? Was Miss Adwell trying to pin the crime on an accomplice? She must have thought I was born yesterday. Well, she was off by nine years, three months and one week. I dared to peek out from behind the stairs, and that's when I saw it.

Miss Adwell was staring straight at Shelter.

'Mabel, it *is* you!' she shrieked. Shelter had never met Miss Adwell before, but the way she ran towards her, tail wagging . . . the way she jumped all over her . . . the way she licked her face and barked with excitement . . . it made me think she must *really* like teachers. Unless . . .

'Oh, Mabel! Where have you been?'

Unless . . .

'You daft pup – I've been looking for you for weeks!'

Unless . . .

'You scared me half to death! I thought something terrible had happened!'

I tried to pretend I didn't realise what it all meant, but I did. Miss Adwell screamed again when I sneezed, and one more time when I crawled out from under the stairs.

'Hugh?' she blurted. 'Hugh Dunnit?'

'Please, Miss,' I said. 'Please don't take my dog.'

9.

Case Closed

And that's the story of how I lost my best friend. I still don't know how Miss Adwell hadn't seen any of my missing dog posters. Then again, *I* hadn't seen the posters Miss Adwell had apparently put up when she was trying to find her lost dog, Mabel. Either way, I hadn't seen this coming. Turned out it wasn't Destiny that brought us to Number 22 Black Swan Spinney – it was Shelter. Like Gran's cough medicine, it was all a bit hard to take in.

'Your dog? Mabel's *my* dog,' Miss Adwell said, cuddling Shelter. 'Also, what are you doing here, Hugh?'

I knew what I wanted to say:

WHY AM I HERE?
I'M HERE FOR JUSTICE.
I'M HERE TO TELL YOU I KNOW WHAT YOU'VE DONE. I'M HERE TO CLEAR MY BEST FRIEND'S NAME AND RIGHT A WRONG.
I'M HERE TO SOLVE A CRIME.

But all the stuff that mattered a minute ago didn't seem to matter any more. All that mattered was happening right here, right now. The truth hurt like a bad tooth. I didn't know what to say, so I just sort of shrugged.

'Wait . . . Hugh, did *you* find Mabel?' Miss Adwell asked. 'Is that what . . . did you bring her back? How did you know she was my dog?'

I felt hot and cold again. Both taps, full blast.

'Is . . . she's really your dog?' I muttered, but I already knew the answer. Shelter was looking at Miss Adwell the way I looked at Shelter. Like she was her best friend.

'As much as Mabel is anyone's dog,' said Miss Adwell. 'She tends to please herself, most of the time. Hang on, have you been looking after her?'

'. . . Sort of,' I said. Then I pretended I had something in my eye.

Miss Adwell said 'Thanks' so many times I started to forget what the word meant. Then she said that if my mum and dad were OK with it, I could come round and take Mabel for a walk every now and then. I said she doesn't do much walking – she likes to play Fetch. Miss Adwell said she never fetches anything – she just chews things to oblivion. I guess she did know my best friend after all.

'I'll see you soon, Shel— Mabel,' I said, and gave her a rub on the top of her head. Then I turned around, sneezed and walked out of the door.

Turns out, this tale comes with a twist. By the time I got home, Mum and Dad had had a change of heart about taking 'Shelter' to the shelter. They were willing to give her one more chance. I said there was no chance, cos Miss Adwell had taken Shelter. I didn't pretend I had something in my eye, then. I sat on the sofa and cried until I'd forgotten what it was like not to be crying.

'I'm so sorry, Hugh,' said Mum, as she and Dad took turns to rub my back. 'I'm not going to pretend that dog wasn't a nightmare, but I know how much she meant to you.'

'Everything probably feels like a sorry soup of sadness right now but in the long run, this is for the best,' added Dad. 'I'll bet Mabel was all out of sorts, not being with your teacher. That's probably why she chewed the house to bits and ate your homework.'

'My homework . . . ?' I muttered with a sniff. I'd never had a best friend before. I wasn't sure if I was ever going to have a best friend again. But I did know that I wasn't about to let the dog, formerly known as Shelter, be remembered as the dog who ate my homework. It had been the toughest case I'd ever taken on. Try as I might, I hadn't found out who'd committed the crime, but I knew one thing for sure – it wasn't – it *couldn't* be my best friend.

I had to face facts in the face – there was only one suspect left . . .

10.

The Only Explanation

'*You?*' Dad blurted.

'Me,' I repeated. '*I* ate my homework.'

'That's the most ridiculous thing I've ever heard,' said Mum. 'And I've heard more than my fair share of ridiculous things today.'

'Well, it's true, and I should know, because I did it,' I said. 'It's the only possible explanation.'

'Ugh, fine,' sighed Mum. 'But please, Hugh, please tell me that's "case closed".'

'I guess . . .' I said with a sniff. 'Case closed.'

'Good lad,' said Dad.

Mum didn't say anything for ages. Truth be told, she didn't say anything so *much* that I swear I could hear her thinking.

'You know, me and your dad, we were never against having a dog,' she said, finally. 'Just preferably not one you find at a bus stop . . . and not one who treats everything we own as a chew toy. When I spoke to the folks at the shelter, they said they had a few dogs that could really do with a good home. They might even have one that doesn't set off your allergies. Maybe, when you're ready, we could go and have a look. What do you think?'

'. . . Get another dog?' I asked.

'Maybe,' said Mum again. 'But, y'know, one that doesn't belong to someone else.'

I wasn't sure what my best friend would think about that. Like Shelter with a tennis ball, I wasn't sure I was ready to let go.

'I'll think about it,' I said.

'Fair enough,' said Dad. 'Now, how about ice cream in front of the telly? D'you have any homework to do for tomorrow?'

'Just geography, but I did it at lunchtime,' I said. 'It's in my bag upstairs.'

But it wasn't.

In fact, my homework wasn't in my bag at all. It was gone. It was as if it had completely disappeared.

Before I knew what was happening, I already knew what was happening – I'd been set up. One homework-related crime? That's a crime. But two? That's . . . actually, I wasn't sure what that was. I eventually settled on *double crime*. Someone was out to get me. It was the only possible explanation.

I realised that only one person could solve this mystery, and that person was looking back at me in the mirror, because I happened to be looking in the mirror when I realised that only one person could solve this mystery.

Everyone was a suspect. But one way or another, I was going to find out who did it.

I had to bring the real culprit to justice. Because I was Hugh Dunnit . . .

. . . And I was on the case.